Busy Babies
Go Swimming

Written by Jane Kemp and Clare Walters

Illustrated by Alex Ayliffe

Collins

An imprint of HarperCollinsPublishers

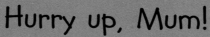

Hurry up, Mum!

What are we waiting for?

Sharing Books From Birth to Five

Welcome to Practical Parenting Books

It's never too early to introduce a child to books. It's wonderful to see your baby gazing intently at a cloth book; your toddler poring over a favourite picture; or your older child listening quietly to a story. And you're his favourite storyteller, so have fun together while you're reading – use silly voices, linger over the pictures and leave pauses for your child to join in.

With *Busy Babies Go Swimming* your baby will see other babies just like him enjoying an outing to the pool. Sing along to the nursery rhymes and point out details like the duck and the ball. Then chat about the last time you went swimming and all the things you needed to take with you.

Books open doors to other worlds, so take a few minutes out of your busy day to cuddle up close and lose yourselves in a story. Your child will love it – and so will you.

Jane & Clare

Jane Kemp   Clare Walters

P.S. Look out, too, for *Busy Babies Go To The Gym*, the companion book in this age range, and all the other great books in the new Practical Parenting series.

AGE
1-2

First published in Great Britain by HarperCollins*Publishers* Ltd in 2000

1 3 5 7 9 8 6 4 2

ISBN: 0-00-136139-2

The Practical Parenting/HarperCollins pre-school book series has been created by Jane Kemp and Clare Walters.
The Practical Parenting imprimatur is used with permission by IPC Magazines Ltd.

Practical Parenting is published monthly by IPC Magazines Ltd.
For subscription enquiries and orders, ring 01444 445555
or the credit card hotline (UK orders only) on 01622 778778.

The HarperCollins website address is: www.fireandwater.com

Printed and bound in Hong Kong.

Busy babies are going swimming!

One... two... three... four tickets, please.

PITTER, PATTER, RAINDROPS,
PITTER, PATTER, RAINDROPS.
I'M WET THROUGH,
SO ARE YOU.

Splish, splash!

Wait for me.

HUMPTY DUMPTY SAT ON A WALL,
HUMPTY DUMPTY HAD A GREAT FALL.
ALL THE KING'S HORSES AND ALL THE KING'S MEN,
COULDN'T PUT HUMPTY TOGETHER AGAIN.

Ready... steady... JUMP!

swish, swish, swish!

Kick, kick, **kick!**

RING-A-RING O'ROSES,
A POCKET FULL OF POSIES.
A-TISHOO! A-TISHOO!
♪ WE ALL FALL DOWN. ♪

Quick, let's catch our toys!

Rub-a-dub-dub

We're warm, dry
and snug.

Swimming makes busy babies hungry
and thirsty, and just a little bit...

...sleepy, too.

Sharing Books From Birth to Five

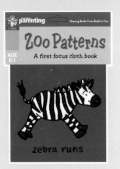
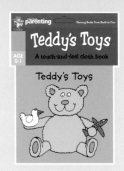

£3.99
0 00 136130 9

£3.99
0 00 136132 5

AGE 0–1

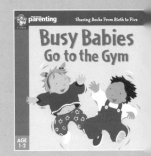

£3.99
0 00 136139 2

£3.99
0 00 136137 6

AGE 1–2

£3.99
0 00 136147 3

£3.99
0 00 136171 6

AGE 2–3

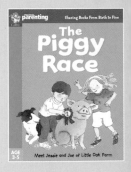

£3.99
0 00 136151 1

£3.99
0 00 136153 8

AGE 3–5

The Practical Parenting books are available from all good bookshops and can be ordered direct from HarperCollins Publishers by ringing 0141 7723200 and through the HarperCollins website: www.**fire**and**water**.com

You can also order any of these titles, with free post and packaging, from the Practical Parenting Bookshop on 01326 569339 or send your cheque or postal order together with your name and address to: Practical Parenting Bookshop, Freepost, PO Box 11, Falmouth, TR10 9EN.